Calico's Cousins

Cats from around the World

Phyllis Limbacher Tildes

ini Charlesbridge

*For my Aunt Tess
and Uncle Earl,
with love*

*A special thanks to
my cat-loving editor,
Yolanda LeRoy*

Published by Charlesbridge Publishing
85 Main Street, Watertown, MA 02472
(617) 926-0329
www.charlesbridge.com

Library of Congress Cataloging-in-Publication Data
Tildes, Phyllis Limbacher.
    Calico's cousins, cats from around the world/
Phyllis Limbacher Tildes.
        p.   cm.
    Summary: Describes various breeds of
cats and where they come from, including the
Abyssinian from Africa, the British Shorthair,
the Japanese Bobtail, and the Maine Coon from
the United States.
    ISBN 0-88106-648-6 (reinforced for library use)
    ISBN 0-88106-649-4 (softcover)
    1. Cats—Juvenile literature. 2. Cat breeds—
Juvenile literature. [1. Cats.] I. Title.
SF445.7.T53   1999
636.8—dc21   98-4011

Printed in the United States of America
(hc) 10 9 8 7 6 5 4 3 2 1
(sc) 10 9 8 7 6 5 4 3 2 1

The illustrations in this book were done in
watercolor on Strathmore 4-ply illustration paper.
The display type and text type were set in
Garamond and Palatino.
Color separations were made by Clarinda Company,
Clarinda, Iowa.
Printed and bound by Worzalla Publishing Company,
Stevens Point, Wisconsin
Production supervision by Brian G. Walker
Designed by Phyllis Limbacher Tildes
This book was printed on recycled paper.

Each breed may have variations in markings and
colors not shown in this book. The descriptions of
breed personalities are very general, and individual
cats' personalities may differ from what is thought
to be typical of their breed.

Hello,
my name is Calico.
I'd like to introduce you
to some of my relatives.

More than five thousand
years ago, humans began
to share their homes
with my wild ancestors.
Today there are many
breeds of domestic cats in
lots of colors, shapes, and
sizes. These breeds were
developed in different
countries but are now
found all over the world.

Let's take a look at my
cuddly cousins and find
out where they came from.

Out of Africa

These two cousins look like ancient cats from northern Africa.

Egyptian Mau

Early Egyptians loved and worshiped cats. Their word for cat was *mau*, which means "to see." The Egyptians believed that cats had the power to see the truth. Alert and agile, the Egyptian Mau can be very attached to its owners, but it may be shy with strangers.

Abyssinian

This elegant cat from Ethiopia has a regal appearance. It is also called the Rabbit Cat because the tips of its fur are a lighter color, just like a wild rabbit's coat. Clever and lively, the Abyssinian is a natural athlete.

Wild for Water

While most cats hate getting wet, these cats from Turkey enjoy playing in water.

Turkish Van

Large and muscular, the Turkish Van will not only wade in water, it often dives right in. Like the Angora, its long fur doesn't tangle and will soon be dry and neat. As loyal as a dog, this intelligent and entertaining cat craves attention and always wants to play.

Turkish Angora

This breed has long been admired for its soft, silky coat. It was named after the Turkish city of Angora, now called Ankara. Delightfully curious, the Turkish Angora likes to climb up high to see what's going on. Although dainty looking, it is an athletic and playful cat that loves to show off.

Posh Pets

These fabulous, fluffy felines were brought
to Europe four hundred years ago.

Persian

Thought to have originated in Persia, which is now Iran, this longhaired breed is one of the most popular in the world. Persians were further developed in Great Britain to become the gentle, glamorous cats we know today. Most pampered Persians love to be admired and enjoy posing for photographs.

True Blue?

Although people call these cats blue, they are really more of a bluish gray.

Chartreux

Known as the smiling cat of France, this strong, stocky breed is friendly and confident. The Chartreux is prepared for harsh weather with a dense, woolly, water-repellent coat that is as soft as rabbit fur. It is a devoted, well-behaved cat that almost never meows.

Russian Blue
The delicate, graceful, and majestic Russian Blue was a favorite pet of Tsar Nicholas I of Russia. This quiet-voiced cat can be shy and sensitive. It is a companionable, home-loving pet that does not like to be left alone.

From Norway's Enchanted Forests

These cats often appear in Scandinavian myths and fairy tales.

Norwegian Forest Cat
Whether fishing in a fjord or frolicking in the snow, these hardy cats love the outdoor life. Equipped with warm, heavy coats, they thrive in cold, wet weather. They are playful, intelligent cats that like to explore.

Classic British Cats

These next four breeds are from the
cat-loving kingdom of Great Britain.

British Shorthair

Descended from cats brought by the Romans two thousand
years ago, this sturdy breed is quiet and affectionate. Admired
for its round features, muscular body, and good nature,
the British Shorthair has long been a popular cat.

Cornish Rex

This cat from Cornwall, England, has a short, curly coat that doesn't shed. Even its eyebrows and whiskers are curled. With such a thin coat, the Cornish Rex needs protection from extreme weather. Mischievous and active, this cat makes an entertaining pet.

No tail? Folded ears?
These cats are curious creatures.

Manx

This cat comes from the Isle of Man, in the Irish Sea. A completely tailless Manx is called a Rumpy. If it has a short stump of a tail, it is called a Stumpy. Legends and fairy tales attempt to explain this rare breed, but tailless kittens first appeared from a genetic mutation several hundred years ago. The Manx is a quiet cat, but it will make a strange trilling sound when excited.

Scottish Fold

With its large, expressive eyes and folded-down ears, this cat is "ear-resistible." The first folded-ear cat, Susie, was discovered on a farm in Scotland in 1961. The Scottish Fold breed was developed from two of her kittens. Peaceable and polite, the Scottish Fold is fond of people and other pets.

Treasures from the Far East

Fortunate indeed are the owners
of the following four cats.

Burmese
The Burmese was developed from a dark-brown
female cat named Wong Mau. Wong Mau came from
Burma, which is now called Myanmar. Highly intelligent,
the Burmese is an easily entertained companion that
can occupy itself for hours with a simple toy.

Birman
The sweet and quiet Birman is known as the sacred cat of Burma. A legend tells how this temple cat received its heavenly blue eyes, golden coat, and snow-white mittens upon the death of a beloved monk. Its lush, silky fur is easy to groom and rarely becomes matted.

These two cats have the style and grace of Asia.

Japanese Bobtail
This thousand-year-old breed from Japan is a symbol of good fortune. Its rabbitlike, pompom tail is unique. As curious as a kitten, the Bobtail wants to be involved with every activity of its owner. It has a musical voice with many sounds and usually insists on having the last word.

Siamese
This sleek and elegant cat is from Thailand, which was once called Siam. The Siamese has a long body, tail, and nose. It has almond-shaped blue eyes, a masked face, and an almost human voice. Intelligent enough to learn tricks, the talkative "Royal Cat of Siam" loves toys and hates to be left alone.

All-American

From friendly, working-class cats to American beauties, these next four cats have many loyal fans.

American Shorthair

This stocky cat is a talented hunter. It was developed from farm cats that came to North America with the first European settlers. The good-natured American Shorthair gets along well with dogs and other cats and makes a "purr-fect" family pet.

Maine Coon

This large cat has a bushy tail like a raccoon's and can weigh twenty pounds or more. The Maine Coon loves the wild outdoors and needs lots of room to roam. A gentle giant, it is easygoing and playful, often teaching itself new tricks. However, it is slow to grow and won't reach full size until it is three to five years old.

These cats are cute and cuddly.

Ragdoll
When held and hugged, the big, blue-eyed Ragdoll will often relax and go limp like a favorite stuffed toy. Even toys need to be handled with care, though, and the Ragdoll appreciates a gentle owner. It is sometimes a little clumsy, but it is a calm and playful pet.

Ragamuffin

This beautiful cat is a type of Ragdoll that comes in a wider range of colors and patterns. Even though its name suggests a raggedy appearance, its thick, silky coat rarely gets tangled.

An Odd Couple

This pair from North America is sure to please cat lovers who seek the unique.

Munchkin

The comical Munchkin has short legs like a dachshund. It runs with a bounding gait like a squirrel and can stand on its hind legs like a prairie dog. Fascinated by small, shiny objects, the Munchkin will often hide them. This playful breed keeps its kittenish personality when fully grown.

Sphynx
Like the Egyptian monument, the Sphynx looks strange and mysterious. However, this almost hairless, slightly wrinkled breed is not from Egypt, but is originally from the United States and Canada. If this Sphynx spent time in the desert, its delicate skin would soon be sunburned. Happy to stay indoors, this loving cat adores people and needs a lot of affection.

You have just met many special, purebred
cats, but I have other cousins too. We are
called domestic longhair or shorthair cats,
and we can be found in countries all
over the world.

Although we're different, we all agree,
There's no place we would rather be
Than curled up for a cozy nap
On someone's warm, inviting lap.

CALICO ~ Domestic Longhair
BENTE ~ Norwegian Forest Cat

HAZOF ~ Abyssinian

MAC ~ Scottish Fold

MISHA ~ Russian Blue

PONGYI ~ Birman

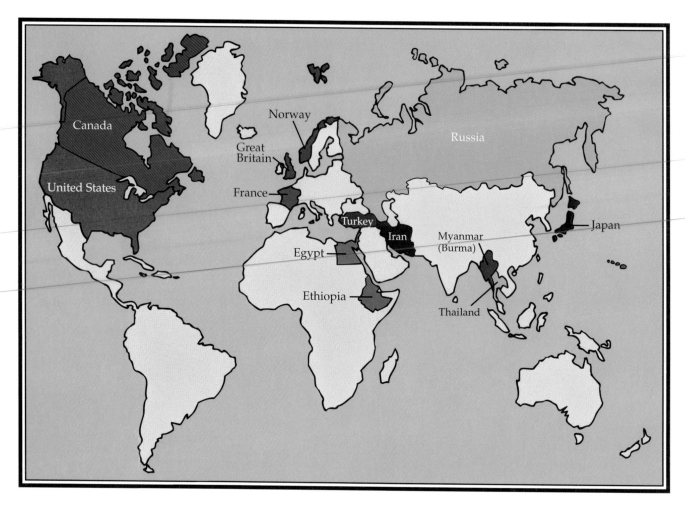

Can you find the country each cat breed came from?

Abyssinian (ab-ih-SIN-ee-un): Ethiopia
Egyptian Mau (ee-JIP-shun MOW*): Egypt
Turkish Angora: Turkey
Turkish Van: Turkey
Persian: Iran
Chartreux (shar-TROO): France
Russian Blue: Russia
Norwegian Forest: Norway
British Shorthair: Great Britain
Cornish Rex: Great Britain
Manx: Great Britain
Scottish Fold: Great Britain
Burmese: Myanmar
Birman: Myanmar
Japanese Bobtail: Japan
Siamese: Thailand
American Shorthair: United States
Maine Coon: United States
Ragdoll: United States
Ragamuffin: United States
Munchkin: United States
Sphynx: United States and Canada

*rhymes with "cow"

Many of these purebred cats are available from breeders in the United States and other countries.
Non-purebred cats and kittens are always looking for homes and can be found in animal shelters everywhere.